A Work of Art

... Holding the penlight with his teeth, Mulder reached out to touch one of the grotesque forms.

"Mulder," Scully called from the other room. "Mulder, what is it? What do you see? Mulder!"

Mulder didn't answer. His hands clawed at the clay face, scraping away at the wet sculpting material. A sick feeling filled him. He had a horrible idea of what he was about to find.

"Tell me what's going on in there!" Scully demanded.

Mulder couldn't. Words deserted him as he peeled away the clay to reveal the form beneath it. The clay had been a cover, a mask really. And under the layers of wet clay was the decapitated head of a man.

READ ALL OF THE X-FILES
YOUNG ADULT BOOKS

*coming soon

Grotesque

A novelization by Ellen Steiber
Based on the television series

THE X FILES™

created by Chris Carter
Based on the teleplay
written by Howard Gordon

HarperEntertainment
A Division of HarperCollinsPublishers

HarperEntertainment
A Division of HarperCollins*Publishers*
10 East 53rd Street
New York, NY 10022-5299

This is a work of fiction. The characters, incidents,
and dialogues are products of the author's imagination and are
not to be construed as real. Any resemblance to actual events or
persons, living or dead, is entirely coincidental.

ISBN 0–06–447179–9

HarperCollins®, ◼®, and HarperEntertainment™ are trademarks
of HarperCollins Publishers Inc.

First Edition, 1999

Printed in the United States of America

Visit HarperEntertainment on the World Wide Web at
http://www.harpercollins.com

For Toby Froud,
who liked this one

With thanks to the glassblowers
at Philbaum Glass:
Jerry Flannery, Jason Metcalf,
Matt Daggliardi, and Romi Epstein

Chapter One

A naked man sat on a raised platform, still as a statue. His lean, sinewy body was posed so that each ribbon of muscle was accentuated by the spotlight above him. He sat perfectly motionless, as if lost in thought, as if he didn't even notice the twenty-five students who stood before their easels, trying to capture his image. Or the one student in the class who drew with a disturbing, almost frightening, intensity.

Peter Gilson, the model, stifled a yawn. It was almost nine o'clock. He wasn't used to working the evening figure-drawing class. Ordinarily he modeled for the afternoon studios. But he was an art student, and the afternoon jobs barely paid for his supplies.

Besides, he liked sitting for Rudy Aguirre, the Adult Extension Program's easygoing professor. A talented artist in his own right, Aguirre was also a gifted teacher. He had a knack for making both the model and the class comfortable, getting the best out of everyone.

Aguirre asked Peter to change his pose, and he shifted so that his right side faced the class. This was Peter's second year modeling, and he was no longer self-conscious about sitting naked with an entire roomful of students staring at him. He knew he had a nice body, and he enjoyed the fact that other people were drawing it, using it as inspiration for their art. His girlfriend liked to tease him, saying that modeling made him vain. Tonight, though, he didn't care about any of that. He was tired and bored. He couldn't wait to get home, take a shower, and crawl into bed.

As the class worked on, the sound of charcoal pencils scratching against sketch pads filled the room with a quiet murmur. Gradually, Peter became aware that something in this particular class felt different from the other drawing studios. He let his eyes sweep the room. The students in the night class were a mixed group, ranging from teenagers just out of high school to gray-haired retirees. All of them seemed to be concentrating intently, working hard. Professor Aguirre was standing beside an older man, gently giving suggestions about proportion. Peter didn't notice anything out of the ordinary.

What he couldn't see was one student who'd taken an easel at the very back of the room. He was a slight man with blue eyes, a thin, bony face, and dark, closely shaved hair. He wore a badly fitting black shirt and looked as though he hadn't eaten or washed in days. His name was John Mostow.

Mostow worked feverishly, almost desperately, a charcoal pencil pinched between his blackened fingers. Sweat beaded his brow. He kept the hand that he wasn't drawing with curled inward, like a bird's talon, tight with tension.

Peter sat still on the platform. His eyes remained vacant, his face expressionless. Until he felt it again. He couldn't even define what *it* was. A difference in energy? In the light? In the way the air was moving through the studio? With the barest of movements, he inclined his head toward the back of the room. Again, he saw nothing but the usual assortment of students sketching, and he moved back into position.

Mostow's eyes darted between his subject and his sketch pad. His breathing was shallow and quick as he drew. Though he was undoubtedly working harder than anyone else in the room, his drawing bore no resemblance at all to the model on the platform. It wasn't even a full figure, but simply a face—if you could call something that monstrous a face. The image on Mostow's drawing pad had a wrinkled brow, huge pointed ears, eyes that slanted up at an impossible angle, and thick black lips showing a hint of razor-sharp teeth. Mostow worked even more furiously as he added shading to the eyes, filling them with a rage and malevolence that matched the expression of the mouth. The image was strangely both human and inhuman. A creature born of the deepest nightmare—its hideous expression at once beautiful and frightening.

Mostow was lost in his drawing, sketching in a frenzy, when suddenly the point on his charcoal pencil snapped. He stopped for a second, frustrated. Then he grabbed a matte knife from the narrow wooden lip at the bottom of the easel. Hands shaking, he hurriedly tried to sharpen the pencil by hand, curling off thin shavings of wood. He winced as the razor slipped and sliced into his finger. His entire forefinger was quickly covered with bright red blood. For the briefest moment he seemed calmed by the cut, fascinated by the sight of it.

It did not occur to Mostow to bandage his finger or even to try to stop the bleeding. He retracted the knife, ignoring the open wound in his hurry to complete his work. He continued to draw with his dripping hand, filling in lines and shadows, making the monster on the page more real with every stroke.

Again the model felt the strange energy in the room. Again he turned his head and eyes just a fraction, toward the back of the class—but this time his view was blocked by Professor Aguirre, standing at a nearby easel, praising a student for his smooth line.

Heedless, Mostow drew more and more frantically, surprised when the blood from his finger seeped into the page, becoming one with the drawing. The monster's eyes were now a bright red. As if blood were everything it saw.

"All right, everyone," Aguirre said, draping a gray wool blanket over the model's shoulders. "That's all for tonight. If you haven't finished, you'll have more time with Peter next week."

Mostow tensed with disappointment and angry frustration. Swiftly, before anyone could see his night's work, he took his drawing from the easel and slipped it into his portfolio. He put the matte knife and pencil in his wooden supply box among the chalks and charcoals, slamming the lid closed. Then he quickly pulled on his coat and started out of the crowded classroom.

Aguirre's eyebrows rose as Mostow rushed past him, a sketch pad under one arm, the other arm awkwardly clutching his portfolio and art supplies. Mostow kept his head down, hunched between his shoulders as though he were trying to make himself invisible. He didn't even see one young man standing directly in front of him, and knocked into him so hard that the student spun around with an indignant "Hey! Watch where you're going!"

"Excuse me," Mostow mumbled, not bothering to stop or even slow down.

Peter stretched on the platform, relieved that the night's session was over. He jumped down, watching Mostow's abrupt exit. He turned to Aguirre, who just shrugged and said, "Guess he's in a hurry."

Two flights down, Mostow was already pushing through the heavy wood-and-glass doors. Outside on the street, he stood for a moment, breathing hard and hesitating, as though he didn't know which direction to take. He looked up along the facade of the old university building till he saw the windows of the art studio. His breath came in ragged gasps. After a moment, he seemed to regain control of himself. He turned to his right, scurrying along the sidewalk and around the corner.

He disappeared into the shadows, his flight witnessed only by a figure on top of the art building. A grotesque stone gargoyle peered down silently from a parapet. Its face was the same as the hideous face in Mostow's drawing.

A short time later, Peter Gilson, now dressed in jeans and a leather jacket, walked down a street on the edge of the George Washington University campus. He still couldn't figure out why the drawing class had felt so strange. Well, it didn't matter now, he told himself. He turned the corner into a poorly lit alley where his red sports car was parked.

His shoulders hunched against the cold, he moved toward the car. He should have worn gloves tonight, he decided as he fumbled for his keys, his fingers numb.

His body tensed as he heard a sound nearby. *Relax*, Peter thought to himself, *it's only a bottle rolling on the ground*. He looked around. There was no one visible in the darkened alley. Everything was completely still.

Then he heard the noise again, and this time he felt a chill go straight down his spine.

"Hello?" he called out nervously. "Is someone there?"

But there was no answer. Keeping his eyes on the alley ahead, Peter continued to search for his keys. He swore softly. They didn't seem to be in either of his pants pockets. Or in his jacket. *This is weird*, Peter thought. *A little too weird*. He couldn't shake the feeling that someone else was close by, watching his every move.

He wasn't entirely wrong. Farther up the alley, a dark figure crouched, watching the young model with a burning intensity. His face was entirely concealed by the shadows. But his hands were smeared with charcoal and blood.

Peter relaxed a little when he finally found his keys in an inner pocket of his jacket. He removed them, then struggled to get the right one into the car door. He couldn't believe this. His hands were shaking so badly that he had to hold the key with both hands. It was crazy to get so spooked. To let his own wild imagination get to him this way.

Then he saw that it wasn't his imagination. There was something wrong. The key wouldn't go in the lock.

With a sigh of exasperation, he bent down to get a better look. He swore again as he saw what the problem was: A thin charcoal pencil had been jammed in the keyhole and broken off, blocking the opening. He tugged on what was left of the pencil, but it held fast.

As Peter stood up, he saw something reflected in the car window: the triangular point of a matte knife blade.

Peter wheeled around, confused and terrified. "No—!" he started to protest. But his attacker didn't listen.

The blade flashed—a lightning-quick streak as the arm that held it reached back. Then the arm drove forward and Peter screamed and fell to the pavement, holding his face. It felt as if it were on fire. Blood was soaking his hands and his scarf.

He screamed a second time as the dark figure dropped down on top of him. The brutal attack continued. The knife slashed him again and again, until Peter Gilson no longer had enough life in him to scream.

Chapter Two

The morning after the attack, John Mostow was in a large, unheated room on the fifth floor of an old factory building. It was both his home and his art studio. He slept on a narrow twin bed, a thin woolen blanket covering his body. He was wearing the same clothes he'd worn to the drawing class the night before.

Beside the bed, a cheap digital clock clicked from 6:29 to 6:30, and a tinny alarm went off. Mostow stirred awake in the darkness, reached an arm out of the blanket, and shut off the buzzer. His eyes blinked open, then squeezed shut again, as if he were suffering from a massive headache.

Without any warning, the front door suddenly exploded inward and a man's voice shouted, "FBI! Don't move!"

Mostow had no time to react. A dozen FBI agents swarmed inside, bearing down on him with flashlights and drawn weapons.

"John Mostow, we've got a warrant for your arrest!" an agent shouted.

Stunned and disoriented, Mostow was pulled roughly from the bed and thrown to the floor. His arms were yanked behind him and his wrists cuffed. He could feel a handgun pressed against the back of his skull.

Agent Greg Nemhauser held up a yellow card and read Mostow his Miranda rights in a quick, grim monotone.

"You have the right to remain silent. Anything you say can and will be used against you in a court of law. You have the right to have an attorney present. . . ."

From the back of the room, Supervising Agent Bill Patterson watched his operation go down. Patterson was a fit, balding man in his early fifties with the steely eyes of a hunter. He stood silently as his crew moved efficiently through the routine of the arrest. Patterson had been working toward this moment for a long time. Now that it was here, he was surprised to find himself experiencing mixed emotions. He was relieved, of course, that Mostow was finally in custody. He also felt curiously let down. They'd tracked Mostow for three years. Now, taking this small, undernourished man as he slept seemed ridiculously easy. Had he expected more of a fight?

"You're hurting me!" Mostow protested as he was jerked to his feet. "You're hurting me!"

"Do you understand each of these rights that I have explained to you?" Nemhauser continued relentlessly. "Do you wish to give up the right to remain silent?"

Mostow answered by biting down hard on Nemhauser's wrist.

Nemhauser screamed in pain and wrenched his arm free, watching as blood pooled in the wound. "He bit me," the young agent said in disbelief. "Sonofabitch bit me like a dog!"

Outraged, Nemhauser wanted to attack the handcuffed man but instead pushed him out toward the door.

"Get him out of here," Patterson ordered briskly, nodding toward Mostow.

"Nemhauser, you okay?" another agent asked.

"Yeah, yeah," Nemhauser answered, his bored tone an attempt to conceal how badly Mostow's attack had shaken him.

Patterson watched as the agents pushed Mostow out the door. Nemhauser, he noted, was continuing to recite Miranda through clenched teeth.

The room was suddenly quiet.

"My God," Patterson murmured as he looked around the squalid studio. Mostow didn't have much in the way of amenities. The bed and clock, a hot plate, a dented pan, and a single plastic cup. Exposed pipes ran up the walls and across the ceiling. But it was the walls that interested Patterson most. They were papered, floor to ceiling, with drawings of gargoyles and grotesques. Full bodies, faces, profiles. Each one a study in horror. Portraits from hell.

Patterson slipped on a pair of latex gloves as he continued to study the images. He pulled one of the smaller sketches from the wall, folding it and placing it in the pocket of his coat.

Then he noticed something at his feet. Mostow's art supply box poked out halfway from under the bed. Patterson pulled it out. It was open, and lying among the charcoal pencils, erasers, and old bottles of black ink was a matte knife, its blade retracted.

Patterson picked up the knife and pushed the blade out of its sheath with his thumb, revealing a thin coat of dried blood on its shiny surface. Patterson smiled. Now he had all the evidence he needed. John Mostow would never see daylight again. This case was finally closed.

Chapter Three

FBI Special Agent Dana Scully removed a teetering pile of folders from one of the chairs in Fox Mulder's office and sat down. Mulder's office, in the basement of the J. Edgar Hoover Building in Washington, D.C., was in its usual state of disarray. The shelves were jammed with books, the counters and chairs covered with files and stacks of magazines. The bulletin board was layered with so many clippings that it was impossible to make out anything except the large poster with lettering that read, I WANT TO BELIEVE. To Scully, her partner's office was chaos. To Mulder, it was the only way he could work.

Mulder made no comment as Scully rearranged his decor, except to say, "It's the file on the top."

Scully picked up the folder labeled MOSTOW and skimmed the contents quickly. At first glance, she couldn't see why this case had been given to Mulder. Mulder specialized in what the FBI referred to as the X-files—a small group of cases having to do with supernatural or alien phenomena. As far as Scully could see, this new case was straightforward murder.

Mulder turned on the slide projector, and John Mostow's mug shot appeared on the screen.

"John Mostow," Mulder said. "Unemployed house painter. Divorced. No children." He walked closer to the screen and studied the killer's troubled face. "Came to the U.S. from Uzbekistan during perestroika."

"That means he arrived in the late 1980s, when Gorbachev was reforming the government of the Soviet Union," Scully said. "If I remember correctly, Uzbekistan became independent from the U.S.S.R. in 1991."

Mulder nodded. "Uzbekistan was the southernmost province of the former U.S.S.R., just north of Afghanistan. Landlocked and only slightly larger than the state of California, it's one of the poorest states of the former Soviet Union. They're still struggling with economic reforms."

"Maybe that's why Mostow immigrated here," Scully said.

"Well, he failed to mention on his INS application that he'd spent the better part of his twenties in a mental hospital."

Scully glanced through the file she held. "Arrested last week for the serial murders of at least seven men."

"And you thought all they produced were great hockey players," Mulder joked.

Scully winced at the quip. Sometimes, she thought, the hardest part about working with Fox Mulder was his bizarre sense of humor.

Mulder clicked the remote. A crime-scene photo flashed on the screen. The victim's lifeless body lay in an alley, twisted at an impossible angle. The face was covered by a mask of crusted blood.

"The crimes took place over a three-year period," Mulder went on. "All the victims were male, ages seventeen to twenty-five."

Scully studied the gruesome projection. "Was there a signature or a defining MO?" she asked.

"Well, according to the medical examiner, there was no evidence of any sexual assault. Death was caused by massive blood loss due to facial mutilation. He also reported the wound pattern among all the victims was identical. It's all there on page three."

Scully flipped to the third page of the report and read aloud, "Both eyes punctured, signature gashes from the corners of the mouth to the ears . . ."

Mulder clicked on a new slide. Scully caught her breath at the grisly image: a man's face so badly cut that there was barely any skin left. Scully had been a medical doctor before becoming an FBI agent and was rarely shaken by blood or gore. Autopsies were even routine for her. But this mutilation was so extreme that it took her a moment to compose herself. At last she said in understatement, "The level of violence and overkill here would suggest the work of a very angry individual."

"Or individuals," Mulder added. "If you count the spirit Mostow says possessed him during the murders."

"Well, possession is a common claim by criminals who have dissociative disorders," Scully said. "It's how they distance themselves from their actions."

"That was the operational opinion," Mulder agreed. "Until last night, when a nineteen-year-old male was killed about six miles from here. He had an identical set of facial wounds."

"A copycat?" Scully guessed.

Mulder shook his head. "According to Assistant Director Skinner, who asked us to look into this case, the details of the mutilations were never released. Only members of the crime team would have had that information, and Mostow's been in custody for five days."

Chapter Four

Scully was behind the wheel as she and Mulder headed west out of D.C. and across the Potomac River. Their destination was Lorton, Virginia, a small town about twenty miles outside Washington. For the FBI, a trip to Lorton usually meant a visit to the D.C. Correctional Complex, an older prison used to house suspects awaiting trial who were considered extremely dangerous. Scully passed a sign warning motorists not to stop for hitch-hikers and knew that the turnoff for the prison was near.

"So," Mulder said as the yellow walls and green copper roof of the institution came into view, "wondering what Mostow will be like?"

Scully thought about the gruesome slides

she'd seen that morning. "Actually, I've been wondering what would make anyone commit a string of murders that vicious."

"Possession by an evil spirit?" Mulder was teasing her, but Scully knew he didn't discount the idea. Mulder didn't rule out anything until he had proof to the contrary—and even then, he sometimes allowed for the strangest theories.

"So you think possession by a spirit is possible?" she challenged him. Scully was trained as a scientist. She didn't believe in anything unless she had logical, concrete proof.

Mulder shrugged. "Numerous cultures have been recording instances of possession for centuries now. In old Japan, they believed it was possible for the spirit of a fox to possess someone and drive him mad. Voodoo rituals *invite* the gods to possess their priests. Native American and Latino peoples tell of people possessed by shape-shifters. And, of course, the Catholic Church tells us that the devil can possess your soul."

"None of that explains away John Mostow's murders," Scully said. She turned onto the narrow paved road that led to the prison. Great clouds of steam from the heating system rose into the winter air. The high yellow walls, as in all prisons, were topped with coils of barbed wire, and the windows were covered with thick steel mesh.

Mulder and Scully showed their IDs at the gate and passed through to the entrance, where they showed them again. Finally, a guard was assigned to take them to John Mostow.

"He's being held in maximum security," the guard explained as he led the two agents through a maze of corridors lined with cells. "He may be a little guy, but no one's going to risk letting him near any of the other prisoners."

The inside of Mostow's cell was dark. The guard slid the cover from the rectangular viewing port, allowing a sharp shaft of light in to pierce the darkness. There was the sound of a key turning in the lock, then the thick steel door swung open.

"Please," Mostow called out in heavily accented English. "The light hurts my eyes."

Mulder and Scully stepped into the cell, their shadows falling over Mostow as he shrank from the light. Behind them, the guard pushed the heavy steel door closed.

Mostow was indeed "a little guy," Mulder saw. He was small and wiry and wearing a white straitjacket. Huddled on the floor next to the cell's narrow bunk, he looked terrified.

Mostow turned his head away, his eyes shut tight. "Leave me alone," he said.

"You have a nice soft bunk, sir," Scully said to the prisoner. "Why aren't you using it?"

Mulder saw the answer at once. "Because he's been working. Haven't you, John?"

Mostow wouldn't meet Mulder's eyes. He was staring at the cement floor. Mulder followed his gaze to the crude outline of a face that had been scratched into the surface with the heel of Mostow's shoe.

It was a monster's face—only vaguely

human—distorted and leering.

"What is it?" Mulder asked, kneeling down to get a better look. "What is this thing?"

"It killed those men," Mostow answered.

"Does it have a name?" Mulder asked, his voice calm. "Is there a name to go with that face?"

"All men know its name," Mostow said.

"What do *you* call it?" Mulder pressed. "Satan? The devil?"

Mostow didn't answer.

"Or maybe it's just the name of your accomplice," Scully suggested.

"I had *no* accomplice," Mostow said.

"You killed all those young men yourself?" Scully asked dubiously.

"*It* killed them! How many times do I have to tell you!"

"Well, *its* fingerprints weren't on the murder weapon—yours were," Scully reminded him. "And *it* won't be tried for seven murders under the death penalty."

"Which is why it laughs at fools like you,"

Mostow said. He turned his glare on Mulder. "And you. Fools who would pretend evil can be brought to heel like a brindle bitch. Or be held by your pathetic gulags. While with a snap of its fingers it makes men lick the greasy floor of hell. Just to see its own reflection."

Mulder felt a chill go through him from the force and conviction of Mostow's words. Or his madness.

Scully, though, was unimpressed. "Is that what it did last night, John?" she asked in a scornful tone. "Snapped its fingers and let another young man die?"

For the first time Mostow met Scully's eyes. "It killed again?" he asked. "Yesterday?"

Neither Scully nor Mulder responded.

Mostow began to tremble violently. "It's found somebody," he said, his voice frenzied. "Somebody new. Just like it found me."

Mulder felt the chill again as his eyes went back to the crude drawing on the floor of the cell. It seemed to be staring right through him.

Behind him, the door to Mostow's cell swung open and an authoritative voice said, "Agent Mulder . . ."

Mulder turned to see two men silhouetted in the corridor of the cellblock. One of them was very familiar, as was his look of disapproval. It was no surprise, really. Mulder knew Patterson had been working on this case. It was only a matter of time before he turned up.

"Can I see you two outside?" Patterson asked.

Scully and Mulder left Mostow's cell, and Patterson pushed the heavy metal door closed behind them.

"This is Agent Greg Nemhauser," Patterson introduced the younger man at his side. One of Nemhauser's wrists, Mulder noticed, was wrapped in a bandage.

Patterson was exactly as Mulder remembered him. He still had the eyes of a hunter, and something in them that always made Mulder think of a tightly coiled spring.

"So what is it this time, Mulder?" Patterson asked, his tone mocking. "Little green men? Evil spirits? Hounds of hell?"

Mulder took Patterson's gibes with a smile. It was easy, really. He'd had lots of practice. "Scully, this is Bill Patterson," he said. "He runs the Investigative Support Unit out of Quantico."

"Yes, I know," Scully said. "Behavioral science—you wrote the book." Bill Patterson was, in fact, a legend among young FBI agents. Patterson had probably developed more criminal profiles than just about anyone. And it was his team that had finally nabbed Mostow. "It's an honor, sir—," she began.

But Patterson cut her off. "Is that what you think, too?" he challenged her. "That the suspect is possessed by some dark spirit?"

"No, not at all, sir," Scully answered truthfully.

"Strange company you keep, then," Patterson said, his eyes sliding toward Mulder.

Nemhauser looked a little unnerved by the conversation, as if he wanted to say something but didn't quite dare contradict or criticize his superior.

Mulder had no such qualms. He smiled. "That's what always amazed me about you, Bill," he said. "How you never fit your own profile. No one would ever guess how really mean-spirited you are." Mulder started to walk away.

But Patterson wasn't done with him. "The arrest of John Mostow is the result of three years of hard work by my unit," he said. "*Three years.* You can imagine that we were very upset by this latest murder. And by the suspect floating this possession theory."

"You think he's got an accomplice, then," Mulder said. "Even though your own profile of Mostow says that he was most certainly working alone."

"My profile led to his arrest," Patterson reminded Mulder. "No, he acted alone. That murder last night was done by a second killer, and he acted alone, too."

"What about these drawings of Mostow's?" Mulder asked. "These gargoyles?"

"Do you know why he draws those?" Patterson demanded. "Did you ask him?"

"I didn't get a chance to," Mulder replied with an ironic smile. He didn't appreciate being yanked out of an interview with a prisoner. And he didn't appreciate Patterson's pulling rank, acting as though he were the only competent agent on the case.

"He says he draws them to keep this demon of his away," Patterson informed them.

"Well, that would make sense," Mulder said. "Historically, that's what gargoyles have been used for—to ward off evil spirits. Like on the eaves of the great European cathedrals— Chartres and Notre Dame—"

"C'mon, Mulder," Patterson interrupted. "I don't need a history lesson. And I don't need *anyone* indulging this guy's story."

Scully watched the conversation with interest. Mulder and Patterson clearly had a history, and it appeared to be a troubled one. Mulder had always been a controversial agent, a maverick, willing to defy his superiors when necessary. Over the years, Mulder had made a number of enemies within the FBI. Scully was starting to get the feeling that she'd just met one.

Mulder, as usual, was not about to back down. "I was asked to look into this case," he told Patterson. "If you've got a problem with that, I suggest you take it up with my superior, AD Skinner."

Chapter Five

Later that afternoon, Mulder and Scully parked outside 1222 South Dakota Avenue in Washington. It was an old red brick industrial building, six stories tall and bordered by a fenced loading yard.

Scully got out of the car and surveyed the structure. "Interesting choice for living quarters," she said. "An abandoned factory." She drew her wool coat tightly around her. The air was damp and bitingly cold.

Mulder glanced around at the neighborhood. It had probably been a major industrial center in the forties. But now the buildings were old and falling apart. A rat scurried along the curb. There was no traffic in this part of the city, no deliveries. "Looks like

Mostow picked himself a good hideout," he said.

The door to the building was secured with an FBI padlock. Scully unlocked it and stepped into a dimly lit hallway. Then she and Mulder took the stairs to the fifth floor.

Mulder was in the lead, setting a brisk pace as he strode toward Mostow's apartment. Ever since they'd left the prison earlier that day, Mulder had seemed troubled, Scully thought. He hadn't said much, but he'd been distracted, vague. Scully had a good idea of what was bothering her partner. Nearly anyone would have been rattled by Patterson's contemptuous attitude. In her usual straightforward way, she decided to confront him with it.

"So you're not going to tell me when your love affair with Patterson ended?"

"Patterson never liked me," Mulder said.

"I thought you were considered the fair-haired boy when you joined the bureau."

"Not by Patterson."

"Why not?" Scully asked.

"I didn't want to get my knees dirty. I couldn't quite cast myself in the role of the dutiful student," Mulder answered.

"You mean you couldn't worship him," Scully translated.

"Something like that, yeah."

They reached the entrance to Mostow's studio. It was a metal industrial door painted red and now sealed with bright yellow police tape. Mulder fished in his jacket for a pocket-knife, then used it to slice through the tape.

"Well, from what I hear there were a lot of guys who *did* worship Patterson," Scully said. "A lot of recruits who joined the FBI because they wanted to *be* him."

"Yeah. Patterson had this saying about tracking a killer," Mulder explained. "'If you want to know the artist, look at his art.' What he really meant was, if you want to catch a monster, you have to become one yourself."

Mulder pushed open the studio door. Nothing had been moved or touched since Mostow's arrest. The blanket on the narrow bed was still rumpled. And the walls were still papered with the sketches of gargoyles.

Scully studied the disturbing yet strangely beautiful images. "In this case, I'd say it served Patterson pretty well," she commented.

"Yeah," Mulder said, gazing at a drawing on the easel. It was all in this one piece: Mostow's unrelenting obsession and his genuine artistry. The other drawings on the walls just confirmed it. The man was haunted, caught in terror and rage, trying to outrun his own demons. Instead, he'd drawn them again and again. Mulder gave a low whistle of amazement. "This guy is definitely some kind of monster," he said.

He continued to stare at the drawing on the easel. The malevolent eyes somehow entranced him. It was as if they held some kind of diabolical secret, and if he only looked at them long and hard enough, he'd have the key to John Mostow.

Scully was examining one of the walls,

wondering what in the annals of psychiatry could possibly explain this, or make sense of it—make John Mostow comprehensible. A dark shape suddenly sprang at her from a high shelf, and she gave an involuntary cry of alarm.

"It's just a cat," Mulder said calmly.

Scully took a breath. "I thought it was one of these pictures coming to life," she admitted. "Our guys must have accidentally locked it in here."

The cat disappeared under the bed. Curious, Mulder knelt down to coax it out. The cat was crouched, watching him with eyes of molten gold. Then it turned and disappeared into a hole in the wall.

"I don't know," Mulder said, straightening. "Looks like he's got his own key to the place."

He pushed the bed away from the wall, revealing another small hole at the baseboard. He bent down and ran his hand over the broken surface.

"There's air coming through here," he told

Scully. "There must be something on the other side of this wall."

Scully was beside him now, knocking on the wall, sliding her hands under the drawings taped to it. She began to pull off the drawings, revealing a thin seam running vertically up the wall.

Mulder was doing the same, finding a parallel seam a few feet away. Together, they peeled away the drawings between the two seams—to reveal a door.

"He's got another room here," Mulder said softly.

The door opened easily. Mulder stepped inside first, sliding his gun out of its holster as he did. Scully waited, then drew her own weapon. She peered into the dark room with trepidation. She would never admit it, but the pictures of the gargoyles and this whole place had her spooked.

"Why don't you wait until we can get some light in here?" she suggested.

"I've got some light," Mulder said, flicking

on a small penlight and holding it up.

He moved past the black cat, who sat watching him from the shadows.

"See anything?" Scully called from the doorway.

"Just more gargoyles."

Mulder's penlight picked out a series of human-size gargoyles.

"Lots of 'em. Sculpted in clay," he added. He moved closer to examine them. They were armless and legless. Busts mounted on metal rods, their faces at eye level. Like the drawings, the sculptures were expertly done, clearly the work of the same disturbed artist.

And then Mulder realized something that sent chills up his spine. Several of the sculptures weren't finished. They were works in progress. Mostow had been in prison almost a week, yet the clay was still wet.

"Why would he keep them in a secret room?" Scully wondered aloud.

Mulder focused his light on one sculpture, a head. The gargoyle's mouth was open, as if screaming. And the mouth was frighteningly real, the teeth slightly uneven, the tongue sticking out, exactly as a real person's might. The sculptor was more of an artist—or more of a monster—than Mulder had realized.

He couldn't help it. He had to know. Holding the penlight with his teeth, he reached out to touch one of the grotesque forms.

"Mulder," Scully called from the other room. "Mulder, what is it? What do you see? Mulder!"

Mulder didn't answer. His hands clawed at the clay face, scraping away at the wet sculpting material. A sick feeling filled him. He had a horrible idea of what he was about to find.

"Tell me what's going on in there!" Scully demanded.

Mulder couldn't. Words deserted him as he peeled away the clay to reveal the form beneath it. The clay had been a cover, a mask really. And under the layers of wet clay was the decapitated head of a man.

Chapter Six

Scully was behind the wheel when they drove
away from the old factory building. Mulder
had barely said a word since phoning in news
of the "sculptures" to FBI headquarters. The
two agents had waited until a forensics unit
arrived to deal with their grisly discovery,
then Mulder had left the scene with unusual
haste.

"I've been thinking about Mostow," Scully
said as she maneuvered through downtown
D.C. traffic toward headquarters. "We don't
have records from the mental institution in
Uzbekistan, but there's a good chance he suffers from multiple personality disorder, a form
of dissociative identity disorder."

"Usually the result of severe or repeated

trauma in childhood," Mulder said, as if reciting from a textbook. Since he had a photographic memory, it was entirely possible that that was exactly what he was doing. Before becoming an FBI agent, Mulder had studied psychology at Oxford University.

"When a child can't physically escape an abusive or traumatic situation, he sometimes 'goes away' in his mind," Mulder went on. "The self dissociates, or 'splits,' into separate or distinct personalities so that it doesn't have to deal with the pain or terror. It's a survival mechanism. The problem is that eventually the survival mechanism becomes reality."

"Exactly my point," Scully said. "It's a well-documented psychiatric condition. Someone with MPD has two or more entities inside him, and each entity may have its own memories and thoughts, its own way of operating in the world. Often these other personalities take control of the individual's behavior. They may not even be aware of each other or of the 'host'—the main personality."

"I'm familiar with all of this, Scully," Mulder said wearily.

Scully stopped at a light and turned to face her partner. "Those other entities—they're called 'alters,'" she said, ignoring his interruption. "And one of the most commonly documented alters is a protector, a personality who exists to protect the host."

"And that's what you think is going on with Mostow?" Mulder asked.

"It's typical of this particular mental illness," Scully reasoned. "It's entirely possible that Mostow committed the murders but won't take responsibility for them because he's actually convinced that a gargoyle—another entity—did it. And then when he draws the gargoyle, he thinks it protects him. Or he might have created the gargoyle because what he does is so horrific that it would destroy him unless he thought it was the work of some supernatural creature."

"Maybe," Mulder said, unconvinced. "That still doesn't explain last night's murder. Or those . . . 'sculptures.' Something besides John Mostow is still out there, Scully. And it's going to strike again."

Although it was nearly midnight, Jerry Morales was still at work in his studio. He was a good-looking young man with short dark hair and a strong, muscular body. He wore a brown T-shirt, jeans, and a gold earring in one ear.

Concentrating intently, he dipped the end of the long metal blowpipe into a ceramic trough filled with molten glass. The liquid was so hot—two thousand degrees—that it glowed white, like a small fiery sun.

Morales had been working with glass for over ten years now, and the careful, practiced motions came easily to him. Sweat streaked his face as he gathered the molten substance, winding it onto the end of the pipe, using a smooth spinning motion to control the viscosity.

He brought the glass over to a stainless

steel table, where he began marvering it—rolling it along the table, applying gentle pressure to shape and cool it.

This was his fourth piece of the night. The one he'd just finished—an ornate vase with an iridescent glaze—hadn't come out at all the way he'd planned. It was definitely a strange piece. But that was what he loved about glassblowing: how it combined physics, chemistry, and art. Sometimes when he was working well, he felt as though the piece itself took over, as if the glass had a will and spirit of its own. At times, it seemed as though the glass would show him what color and what shape it was meant to take.

He blew into the pipe gently, then covered the end of it with his finger, watching as the air inside the heated pipe moved to the other end to expand inside the glass, giving it a rounded form. This one would be a bowl.

He put the metal pipe, with the blown glass still attached, into the furnace to reheat it and glanced up at the clock on the wall. He usually didn't work this late, but he had a show opening that weekend with major buyers coming in from the LA galleries.

He kept working the glass, wondering why he hadn't at least turned on the tape deck when Daryl left. Daryl, his studio partner, was there most evenings, but tonight he'd left at nine. The workshop seemed strangely empty without him.

A sound from the other end of the studio caused Morales to stop. He was working by the light of the glowing red furnace. The rest of the room was dark. He listened attentively, his eyes scanning the dimness. Everything looked normal: the bookcases with their rows of reference works; the cabinet that held the rods of color; the metal shelves and carts loaded with supplies and finished pieces. Row after row of vases, pitchers, bowls, and goblets, each one a delicate swirl of transparent color.

For a long moment Jerry stood motionless, aware that he was losing precious time. The glass was cooling. He ought to be shaping it, yet he remained frozen. Listening. The only sounds were the rushing hiss of the gas furnace—and his own heartbeat. This was crazy. He was making himself paranoid. He waited, then, sure that he hadn't heard anything, went back to work, dipping the blowpipe into the trough to gather more glass.

Far across the room, a figure stepped out from the shadows. It moved silently past the shelves filled with glass pieces. Its hand pushed the blade of a matte knife out of its sheath.

The uneasy feeling wouldn't go away. Jerry turned again—and this time he saw his visitor. At first he thought it was a joke. Someone in a costume, maybe an artist from one of the other studios in the building. The guy who did the big abstract oil paintings was always throwing all-night parties—maybe this was one of his guests. But the glassblower's expression changed from disbelief to horror as he saw the blade glinting red in the light from the furnace.

He raised the metal pipe, trying to block the attack, but he didn't have a chance. The knife slashed down, and the glassblower's anguished screams echoed through the empty building.

Moments later, the studio was quiet again. All that was left beside the young man's body was a glowing ball of molten glass.

Chapter Seven

Jerry Morales lay motionless on a bed in the intensive care unit of George Washington University Hospital. Only his eyes, the end of his nose, and his lips could be seen through the thick bandages that covered his face. Clear plastic tubes and assorted wires connected to a series of electronic monitors maintained his tenuous hold on life. In the eight hours since the attack, he'd almost gone into cardiac failure twice.

Agent Greg Nemhauser stood just outside the room, finally having snagged the attention of one of the victim's many doctors. "What's his prognosis?" Nemhauser asked.

"Prognosis?" the doctor echoed, her voice filled with disbelief. "Given the last eight hours the man is just lucky to be *alive*."

"Thank you, Doctor," Nemhauser said stiffly. He turned as he saw Dana Scully at the far end of the corridor, moving toward him urgently. "Agent Scully—"

"I just checked with Forensics," she reported. "They've turned Mostow's studio upside down. There don't appear to be any more bodies."

"How many were recovered?" Nemhauser asked.

"Five," Scully reported grimly. "All of them dismembered. All young men whose faces were mutilated . . . just like the latest victim, so I hear."

"At least this one's still alive." Nemhauser led her into Jerry Morales's hospital room.

"Same signature facial mutilation," he said as he stood over the young glassblower. "Right down to the choice of weapon, by the look of it."

"What does Patterson have to say?" Scully asked.

"I haven't spoken with him yet," Nemhauser admitted. "But I have to bet he's going to come around to the idea that someone's working directly with Mostow."

"I'd have to agree with that theory," Scully said.

"What does Agent Mulder think?" Nemhauser asked.

"He thinks finding the secret sculpture gallery isn't going to do him any favors with Patterson," Scully said honestly. She thought it was crazy that Mulder even had to worry about such a thing, but his personality clash with Patterson couldn't be ignored.

"Between you and me," Nemhauser confided, "I think Patterson secretly went to Skinner and requested that Mulder be put on this case."

"He requested him?" Scully echoed, surprised.

"I've been working with Patterson for three years on this," Nemhauser told her. "And the case just about killed him—until we finally got a break and arrested Mostow. But then this first copycat murder, you know . . . it really threw him for a loop."

"Mulder's under the impression that Patterson never thought too highly of him."

"That's just Patterson," Nemhauser assured her. "Late at night, with a couple of beers in him, he starts telling me Mulder stories. How he's some kind of cracked genius."

Scully nodded, registering the irony of this. Then she noticed the butterfly bandage on Nemhauser's arm. "Stitches," she said. "What happened?"

"Mostow, if you can believe it. He actually bit me during the arrest."

"How's our victim?" asked a brisk voice behind them.

They both turned to see Patterson entering the ICU. He was stone-faced, his eyes fixed on the patient.

"Has he been able to ID his attacker?" Patterson asked.

"The doctors say it's still too early to even

try," Nemhauser answered. "Not in his condition. They're not even sure he's going to make it."

In the hospital bed, Jerry Morales turned his head, struggling to swallow through the thick tube in his throat.

Patterson seemed oblivious to this. He glared at Scully. "Where's Mulder?"

"He told me he was going to see what he could find out about those drawings of Mostow's," she answered.

"What's he looking for?" Patterson's tone made it clear that he thought Mulder was wasting precious time.

"I think the same thing you are, sir," Scully replied evenly. "A second killer."

The glassblower's eyes opened slightly. Three strangers stood talking at the end of his bed. His eyes were going in and out of focus, and there was a white haze around everything. There was a fourth person, too. Someone in a white coat.

The doctor ignored Morales's visitors. She

was watching the monitors spike as his eyes opened briefly and he struggled to breathe through his mouth. Then his eyes closed again and the monitors settled.

The doctor stroked Jerry's hair as he struggled to breathe. She turned to the three FBI agents and said crisply, "I think you should take this conversation outside."

Chastened, the three agents left the room. Sitting beside the bed, the doctor continued to gently stroke her patient's hair. He was still struggling, she saw, fighting for his life.

She clasped the young man's hand in her own, as if she could hold him back from death. "Stay with us," she told him. "Stay with us."

Chapter Eight

Mulder didn't even notice when daylight turned to dusk, and dusk to darkness. He remained exactly where he'd been since early that morning: in one of the reading rooms of the Georgetown University library. The table he was working at was piled high with reference books. He was beginning to feel as if he'd gone through every book in the stacks.

He looked up and rubbed his eyes, glancing through the arched doorway into the next room. The library was nearly deserted. Still, it wasn't a bad place to work late, he thought. The library was one of the older buildings on campus, and had a warmth that some of the newer structures lacked. Brass reading lamps with green shades lit each of the tables. An old-fashioned wooden card catalog stood at the back of the room.

Mulder returned his attention to the open book in front of him. There was a black-and-white illustration of a winged gargoyle on Chartres Cathedral. He read the text beneath it:

> . . . the word is from the French gargouille, the name of a medieval dragon which prowled the river Seine, whose horrible image became the symbol of the souls of the condemned turned to stone. Or of the devils and demons of the underworld spared eternal damnation.

Mulder turned the page and continued reading.

> The gargoyle is also seen as the embodiment of the lesser forces of the universe who inspired dread and the threat of our own damnation. They were the ushers into hell or into the realm of our own dark fears. . . .

Is this getting me any closer to understanding John Mostow? Mulder asked himself. He thought back to his studies at Oxford. Like most clinicians, he was familiar with the signs and symptoms of many forms of mental illness, yet he'd never come close to understanding what drove any human to go to Mostow's extremes. The strange thing was, when they'd visited Mostow yesterday, it was almost as if the prisoner wanted them to understand, as if he was trying to tell them. Maybe *he* was the one who was crazy for trying to make sense of Mostow's rantings. And yet he couldn't just let it go. . . .

Hours later, Mulder was still staring at illustrations of various horrific demons. One fact taunted him. Gargoyles became popular on churches at a time when each cathedral was supposed to be a "sermon in stone" whose meaning could easily be read by an illiterate population. The intention was that anyone could just look at the gargoyles and know exactly what they were—whether protectors or creatures from hell itself, Mulder could only guess.

He took out one of Mostow's drawings and compared it to the engravings in the reference book. It was not dissimilar.

The image of the gargoyle surfaces again and again, as if resurrecting itself by its own will through tortured human expressions . . . almost as if it existed, haunting men inwardly so that it might haunt mankind for eternity. . . .

. . . as it must have haunted John Mostow, Mulder wrote. He heard footsteps in the library but ignored them, lost in his thoughts. *But what impulses moved him to kill? Is this evil something born in each of us,* he wondered, *crouching in the shadow of every human soul, waiting to emerge . . . a monster that twists our will to do its bidding? Is this the monster called madness?*

His eyes started to drift closed and his head nodded. Unaware, he fell asleep, his head resting on one of the open books.

"The library's closing up in a few minutes," Patterson said crisply.

Mulder woke with a start. His former supervisor bent down and flipped through one of the books spread out on the library table. "So . . . *this* is how you're looking for the second killer?" Patterson's voice was etched with sarcasm.

Mulder turned to him but said nothing. No matter what he answered, Patterson would only shoot him down. He'd always been a relentless hunter. And so Mulder had learned long ago that it was best not to give Bill Patterson a target.

"Tell me, Mulder," Patterson said. "What do you really expect to find here?"

"I'm not sure yet," Mulder said honestly.

"But you must have some idea, some kind of theory. . . ."

"I've got a few theories," Mulder admitted. "I'm just trying to stitch them together right now."

"With your face stuck in a library book?"

"You said it yourself, Bill. 'If you want to know the artist, look at his art.' I'm finally agreeing with you."

Patterson's eyes narrowed with contempt. "I know where you're going with this, Mulder. Because I've been there myself. So I can tell you, you're wasting your time."

"Then maybe you can also tell me why this man was compelled to draw and sculpt the same face again and again? Why he's still doing it now?"

"Because he's insane," Patterson answered. He picked up Mostow's sketch and crumpled it. "This is nothing but the scrawling of a madman."

Mulder refused to believe that was all there was to it. Something Mostow had said in the prison cell bothered him. "Mostow said this thing wants to see its own reflection. Which means it needs humans who will mirror or embody its own nature. He said—"

"Mostow has said everything except what I need to hear," Patterson broke in impatiently.

"The name of his accomplice."

Mulder considered the drawing on the table. "Unless he's telling the truth."

"About being possessed?"

Mulder didn't answer and Patterson shook his head. "I have to tell you," Patterson said. "I'm really disappointed in you."

Mulder had heard that line so many times it was almost funny. "Well, I wouldn't want to disappoint you by not disappointing you," he assured his former supervisor.

Patterson couldn't resist getting in the parting shot. "After all this time, I thought maybe you'd finally put your feet back on the ground. Clearly, I was mistaken."

With that, Patterson walked away, leaving Mulder wondering why, even when he knew better, he could still be stung by Patterson's criticisms.

Mulder stood up slowly and stepped away from the table to stretch his stiff shoulders. He drifted over to the window and peered thoughtfully out at the darkened street below.

Something on the other side of the arched window caught his attention. A stone gargoyle was hunched over the eaves only a few feet away. It distinctly resembled one of Mostow's creations. And it appeared to be looking directly at Mulder. Haunting him. Perhaps hunting him. Was it just a piece of stone, or something much more powerful?

Mulder stared back at the creature, his own eyes darkening.

Chapter Nine

Scully knocked on the door of Mulder's apartment and waited for him to answer. She told herself to be patient. After all, it was nearly eleven at night. He was probably asleep, so it might take him a few minutes to wake up and get to the door. If he was there, that is. Scully hadn't seen or heard from her partner in two days. The last she'd been told about him was that Patterson had seen him at the Georgetown library yesterday. She knocked again, this time more loudly. She had an awful feeling that Mulder wasn't there at all.

"Mulder?" she called through the door. "Mulder, it's me."

Still no answer. Worried now, Scully decided

she couldn't risk waiting any longer. She took out the key that Mulder had given her and opened the dead-bolt lock.

The door creaked open.

"Mulder?" she called again.

But there was still no answer from within. She entered tentatively and turned on the light. The living room looked the way it always did. Mulder's minimalist decorating skills had made the room functional but far from cozy.

The living room was like Mulder's home office. He had a desk, a computer, a couch, and more of his endless stacks of files and reference books. Scully crossed the room and turned on a floor lamp.

Her eyes widened in surprise as she saw one of Mostow's charcoal gargoyles staring back at her, eerily lit by the spill of light from the lamp. The drawing had been taped to the wall at a slightly oblique angle.

Scully recoiled in horror as she realized that this was only one of many drawings. She looked around the room, almost dizzy with what she saw. Mulder had completely covered all four walls of his living room with Mostow's drawings and gruesome photos of his sculpture studio. The room had become a collagelike shrine to the predator and his prey.

If you want to know the artist, look at his art. What was this, Scully wondered—Mulder trying to go Patterson one better?

She stepped closer to the wall, more than a little frightened by what she saw. Mulder was a dedicated agent, and one of the best criminal analysts in the Bureau. It wasn't unusual for him to immerse himself in a case until it was solved. But this went above and beyond his usual devotion to his job. Way beyond.

Scully's gaze lingered on the largest of the gargoyle drawings. It seemed to embody all of Mostow's madness: a creature driven by terror and rage, a monster hungry for blood and destruction. Scully gave a slight shiver. If she didn't know better, she'd swear it was about to spring off the page.

• • •

Mulder was once again in the dim, depressing studio that Mostow had called home. He'd gone another day without a shower, a razor, or a hairbrush. Or very much sleep. According to the digital clock on Mostow's nightstand it was 12:14 A.M. Mulder wasn't even sure why he was here, except that he felt drawn to the studio. After all, the second killer had not only killed, he'd then found his way into Mostow's studio to make his "sculptures." Which meant that if he was still out there murdering young men, there was a good chance he'd return again.

Mulder continued along the perimeter of the room, studying the gallery of charcoal drawings that remained on one wall. He was struck both by the repetition of the images and by the subtle differences among them. Though Mostow had drawn the same face over and over again, the gargoyles' bodies were endlessly varied. They were all monsters straight out of myth. One had bat wings and scales like a fish. Another had an eagle's talons and a bull's horns. Each drawing seemed to reflect a different nightmare. . . .

Mulder rubbed the back of his neck. That line of thought certainly wasn't leading anywhere constructive.

The drawings held the key to the case. Mulder was convinced of it. There was something about them, *in* them—and if he could only understand what it was, then he'd understand what Mostow understood and know who the second murderer was. The question was: Could he ever fathom what possessed John Mostow without letting it possess *him*?

Mulder studied another of the grotesques. He looked at it closely for a moment, then reached out to touch it. Tentatively at first, then tracing his fingers along the contours of its terrible face. . . .

One hour later, Mulder had moved into the room that Mostow had used as a sculpture studio. An industrial skylight flooded the space with eerie blue light. Mulder had rolled up his shirtsleeves and was standing over a bowl filled with muddy water. Methodically, he dipped his hands into the water and then began shaping the basketball-size mound of clay that was sitting on the wooden pallet in front of him.

Mulder's fingers ran over the clay's rough topography, then began to knead it. Then to work it. As others in this room had done before him, he worked the clay with a singular, disturbing intensity that was almost violent. . . .

Mostow's digital clock read 3:35 A.M. Mulder was sleeping in the painter's narrow bed, his hands crusted with clay, his coat serving as a blanket. Looking not unlike Mostow in the moments before his arrest.

As Mulder slept, a shadow fell across his face. An icy wind swept into the room, and a rotting smell fell like a cloak over the bed.

Something was in the studio, and it was watching him.

Groggily, Mulder opened his eyes, turning his head to one side, then looking up. A dark figure stood over him. Mulder got only the briefest glimpse before the shape raced off. He blinked, wondering for just a second if what he had seen could possibly be real: a man's body, wearing a man's black pants and black jacket. But the fingers of each hand ended in long curving claws. And the creature's face was straight out of one of Mostow's drawings.

Mulder scrambled out of the bed. Not even stopping to grab his coat, he took off in pursuit. Ahead of him the figure raced into the dark hallway, its features hidden from view.

By the time Mulder reached the corridor, the creature was gone—swallowed up by the shadows of the old factory. Frustrated, Mulder stood still, trying to pick a direction. Then he heard the distant sound of footsteps on the floor above.

Mulder charged up the stairs. He found himself in a graveyard of industrial equipment, silhouetted in the moonlight. An eerie wind whistled through the cracked windows, and a faint trace of the rotting smell filled the air.

The gargoyle was definitely on this floor. Mulder heard its heavy footsteps somewhere in front of him. He took off after it, forcing himself into a sprint, dodging pipes and ducts. It was like running an obstacle course in the dark.

Ahead of him, he saw the figure starting up a ladder. Mulder reached the ladder and pulled himself up, two rungs at a time, the metal cold beneath his hands.

The ladder led to a long catwalk with yellow steel railings. The narrow walkway was shaking with the gargoyle's steps. Mulder pounded after the creature, breathing hard. The catwalk zigzagged around massive pipes, but Mulder was gaining. Until the gargoyle disappeared over the rise at the end of the walkway.

Mulder followed, then stopped suddenly. They were on the top floor of the building but the dark figure was no longer in sight. Mulder looked around and drew his gun from the holster at his waist.

Mulder knew better than to think the monster had vanished. He edged forward cautiously, listening and watching intently for any sign of the creature. He hadn't taken more than a few steps when the gargoyle stepped out of the shadows and struck him.

Mulder went down, screaming as the creature's claws raked his face. He reached up and felt blood running from a gash beneath his eye. Shakily, Mulder got to his feet. He never had a chance to fight back. The creature struck again. This time its blow sent Mulder flying into the air and over the edge of a railing.

He landed on a floor ten feet below. He hit hard but was lucky enough to land on an old tarp that somewhat cushioned his fall. He lay still for a moment, dazed and aching, the wind knocked out of him. Blood flowed freely from the cut on his face.

When he could breathe again, Mulder slowly got to his feet. Everything was still, as if the entire city had fallen silent. There was no sound or movement. The creature was gone. Mulder thought of the grotesque face he'd glimpsed so briefly, and wondered exactly what it was he'd just seen.

Chapter Ten

The static squawk of a police radio cut the night, and the whirling lights of patrol cars painted the cracked, grime-covered windows of the abandoned factory red and blue. It was just after four in the morning. The sky was still pitch black, the air frigid. To the cops gathered at the old brick building, the winter night seemed endless.

Scully stood in the stairwell, watching as a paramedic bandaged Mulder's cut. *Mulder looks terrible,* Scully thought. His eyes had a feverish glint, and his body was nearly vibrating with tension. He sat silently, not bothering to offer a word of explanation. What had happened to him? she wondered. Why was he being so secretive? Was this all because he felt he had to prove himself to Patterson?

After checking out Mulder's apartment, Scully had driven back to headquarters, thinking Mulder might be in his office. But it was empty. Finally Scully had gone to the only other place she could think of: John Mostow's studio.

Sometimes, Scully thought, *Fox Mulder is as much of a mystery as any of our cases.* She had no problem with his occasional need to work alone, but this was getting ridiculous. He was in seriously dangerous territory here, and she wasn't even sure if he was aware of it. "Mulder—," she began.

"I'm fine," he said flatly. "You didn't have to come after me."

"You weren't at home or in your office," Scully explained.

Mulder acted as though he hadn't heard a word she'd said.

"I didn't know where you were," she went on, wanting him to understand. "I kept trying your cell phone, but you didn't answer."

"It was turned off," Mulder said.

"You turned your phone off?" Scully asked, her concern rapidly changing to frustration. "Why do you even bother carrying it?"

But Mulder didn't answer.

The paramedic started to put his first-aid supplies back in his kit. "You're all set," he said to Mulder. "You'll want to see a doctor sometime tomorrow, in case of infection."

Mulder nodded curtly, then grabbed his coat from Scully and moved off without acknowledging either of them.

"Thanks," Scully said to the paramedic, giving him an apologetic look.

"Sure," he replied.

Scully hustled after her partner, catching up with him as he strode purposefully down the flight of stairs toward the exit.

"Mulder, you still haven't told me what you were doing here."

He put on his overcoat. "I was working," he replied.

"At three-thirty in the morning?"

Mulder didn't bother to reply. He pushed

open the outer door and headed toward his car. The area surrounding the factory was still bustling with cop cars. Scully practically chased Mulder through the yard. At first, she'd been relieved when she found him and realized he was all right, but now she was more worried than ever. And she wasn't about to let him get away without some kind of explanation.

"Mulder, I haven't seen or spoken to you in almost two days now," she told him. "You haven't returned any of my calls—"

"This thing exists, Scully," he broke in. "It's real."

"*It?*" Scully echoed. "What are you talking about?"

"Whatever keeps killing those young men," Mulder replied. "The thing that possessed John Mostow and now is inside someone else."

Scully had no patience for Mulder's supernatural explanations now. This case was absolutely clear and it was time Mulder saw it. "Mostow killed those men, Mulder. He suffers from multiple personality disorder, and *he* may believe it was a 'thing' that committed the murders, but they were his own actions. And now, out of some sick alliance, another person is continuing where he left off."

Mulder turned to face her. "Whatever attacked me . . . wasn't a person."

Scully stared at him, knowing he was telling the truth, but also knowing he was wounded and exhausted. He probably hadn't eaten or slept in days. *Anyone's mind can play tricks in that state,* Scully told herself.

She began to tread more carefully. "Well, did you actually see it?"

Mulder answered her with silence.

Scully hated to say it but had to. "Mulder, maybe you were just seeing what you wanted to see—"

"What makes you think I would want to see that?" he shot back. "I didn't imagine it, Scully."

Both Mulder and his partner were oblivious to the presence of Patterson and Nemhauser, who had just arrived.

"Listen to yourself, Mulder," Scully urged him. "Listen to what you're saying. You're starting to sound like—"

She stopped herself and sighed as they reached Mulder's car. Challenging him wouldn't do any good; it would only make him defensive. And she wanted him to understand. When she spoke again, her voice was calmer. "Look, when I couldn't reach you, I went to your apartment. I saw your new wallpaper."

Mulder ignored her, fishing the keys out of his pants pocket and opening his car door.

"Don't you realize what's happening here, Mulder?" Scully said. "He is testing you. He's the reason you were assigned to this in the first place, and he's pushing all your buttons."

Mulder hesitated before getting into the car. "Patterson?" he asked quietly.

"He requested your involvement through Skinner's office," Scully told him. "I checked the three-oh-two myself."

Mulder nodded evenly, keeping his thoughts to himself, then he climbed in behind the wheel.

"Mulder," she said wearily, "where are you going?"

But her partner was not answering any more questions. Scully watched as he closed the door, cranked the ignition, and drove off, leaving her baffled and exhausted.

More than ready to go home, Scully turned toward her own car. Patterson and Nemhauser were standing a short distance away. The two agents were talking, but Scully had the definite feeling that Patterson had witnessed her argument with Mulder. She strode toward him, trying to contain her rising anger.

"So how's Mulder holding up?" Patterson asked.

The question itself was proof to Scully that she was right. She didn't answer, but asked instead: "Sir, can I have a minute?"

"Of course," Patterson said.

"In private?" Scully asked.

Patterson nodded to Nemhauser, who moved off. The supervisor turned to Scully, his manner brisk. "What's this about?"

"Maybe you can tell me," Scully said. "I'm curious as to what you're doing concerning Agent Mulder."

"I'm afraid I don't know what you're referring to," Patterson said.

But Scully refused to be put off. "I think you do, sir," she said. "I think you knew exactly how Agent Mulder would respond when you brought him in on this case."

Patterson stared at her, poker-faced.

"You did request him, didn't you?" Scully pressed.

"If you're concerned about Agent Mulder's conduct or behavior, maybe you should take that up with him."

"You know I already have," Scully said, her intense eyes boring into his.

"Then what do you want from me?"

"I just want you to be honest with me

about what you're trying to do. Is this some kind of payback for what happened eight years ago? Because Mulder quit the Investigative Support Unit?"

"My motivations aren't that petty," Patterson assured her.

"Then why?"

"I asked for Mulder because"—there was a vulnerability in Patterson's voice that Scully hadn't heard before—"I want to close the book on this godforsaken case once and for all."

Scully felt a wave of shock go through her. Patterson's motives were the exact opposite of what she had suspected. "And you knew he could help you solve it."

Patterson looked at her as if to say, "We both know Mulder can solve it." But what he actually said was, "My advice to you, Scully, is to let Mulder do what he has to do. Don't get in his way. And don't try to hold him back. Because you won't be able to."

Chapter Eleven

Scully watched as Patterson moved off. His explanation of why he'd drawn Mulder into the case hadn't reassured her. In fact, it left her more worried than ever. Whoever was still committing the murders had the legendary Bill Patterson so scared that he'd called in help. And he knew full well that Mulder, his secret weapon, might not come out of the case alive.

Scully moved wearily toward her car. It was definitely time to go home. She was thoroughly exhausted and no closer to solving the case than she had been three days ago. All that had changed was that she was closer to losing her partner. Possibly for good.

She unlocked her car door and got inside. Turning the key in the ignition, she started the engine. Then, as she reached out to close the door, she saw something that stopped her—something metallic embedded in the front tire of the squad car parked just a few feet away.

Scully reached over and grabbed her flashlight from the glove compartment. She got out of her idling car and snapped on the light as she moved toward the squad car. Curious, she hunkered down to examine the tire more closely. A sliver of metal protruded from the thick rubber tread.

Scully removed a handkerchief from the pocket of her coat and used it to delicately extract the metal sliver.

It was a triangular blade from a matte knife, crusted with blood. Scully examined the blade for a moment, then craned her head beneath the wheel well, sweeping her flashlight beam beneath the squad car.

Her eyes followed the path of the beam, and she saw one broken half of the knife handle. She spotted the other half a few feet away.

Inside the warden's office of the D.C. Correctional Complex, Mulder awaited clearance for his unscheduled visit. The agent was ashen-faced, unshaven, and running on almost no sleep. The bandaged cut under his right eye burned like a small fire. He knew he ought to be home in bed, but he had to answer the question that had been haunting him since last night's attack. And there was only one person who might know the answer: John Mostow.

At last the paperwork was approved and Mulder was buzzed through a steel door. He followed a guard to Mostow's cellblock, moving down dark corridors lined with shadowy compartments. Though he kept his eyes fixed straight ahead, Mulder could feel the other prisoners watching him from their cells, violence contained in their silent stares. He wondered how many of them had been visited by a creature like the gargoyle.

The guard stopped in front of Mostow's cell and opened the heavy steel door for Mulder. This time Mostow was sitting on his bunk. He still wore the white straitjacket. His eyes were red-rimmed but glittered with a feverish intensity. His face was covered with a light sheen of sweat. He looked smaller to Mulder, as if it had been days since he'd eaten. He watched suspiciously as Mulder approached him.

"Why didn't it kill me like it killed the others?" Mulder demanded.

Mostow looked away, refusing to answer.

"Why did it let me live?"

Finally, Mostow said, "Even if I could tell you why, you would not understand."

Mulder knelt in front of him, staring into his eyes. "Then help me to understand, John."

"Please," Mostow said. "Go away!"

"No," Mulder said, determined to get some answers this time. "You have to help me go deeper. You have to help me get inside its head like it got inside yours. So I can understand what it wants—"

"It wants what it wants!" Mostow's voice had an edge of hysteria to it, one that matched the desperation Mulder felt.

"It wants to kill innocent young men by carving up their faces?"

Mostow was shaking with terror now. "You have felt its hunger? Felt your bones rattled by its frozen breath?"

Mulder met Mostow's terrified gaze, wordlessly answering him.

"So you know," Mostow said, his voice suddenly quiet. "*Nothing can be done.*"

"Unless I find it," Mulder told him.

Mostow's tone became contemptuous. "Then what will you do?" He got to his feet, inching away as if Mulder were the madman.

Mulder's voice was almost a whisper. "Just tell me how to find it, John."

"No!"

"Just tell me how to find this thing."

Mulder was on his feet now, stalking Mostow in the small cell.

"You can't find it!" Mostow insisted.

Mulder struck him hard, a blow to the chin that knocked Mostow to the floor. Mostow cried out, then slumped against the cell wall.

Mulder knelt again, his hands closing around Mostow's neck.

Finally, Mostow choked out an answer. "Only *it* can find *you*."

Mulder released him and stood up, sickened by his own violent outburst. Something in the man's glittering gaze gave Mulder the eerie impression that Mostow was able to look straight through him and see a truth that Mulder himself couldn't. "Maybe," Mostow said, "it already has."

Chapter Twelve

Inside the Latent Fingerprint Section of the FBI's Sci-Crime Lab, Agent Sarah Sheherlis switched off the overhead lights. Sheherlis was in her forties, a woman with an unguarded, intelligent presence. She was, in Scully's opinion, an excellent scientist: a precise and patient technical analyst who was open to all possibilities.

Sheherlis walked over to the workbench where Scully was examining the two halves of the matte knife under a magnifier. Scully had deliberately brought the knife and blade to Sheherlis because she was one of the FBI's finest technicians. Not only could she find things others had missed, but Scully had never known her to be wrong.

Sheherlis offered Scully a pair of filtered goggles, identical to the pair hanging around her own neck.

"First time up, I struck out," she said to Scully. "All three pieces were clean," she explained. "But on my second try I got lucky."

Sheherlis raised her goggles to her eyes, and Scully did the same. As Sheherlis turned on a wandlike device with an ultraviolet tube along its length, Scully twisted off the magnifier light. The violet light reflected eerily in their goggles.

"I dusted the blade with redwop. . . ." Sheherlis said.

"I'm sorry?" Scully responded, not following.

"'Powder' spelled backwards," the technician explained. "That's what we call the fluorescent lycopodium."

Sheherlis directed the UV wand over the knife blade, and Scully peered through the magnifying lens.

A crescent print glowed red on the surface of the blade.

"Looks like a partial index," Scully said.

"And on the left half of the handle, almost a full thumbprint," Sheherlis added. She adjusted the UV wand over the handle, revealing an articulated thumbprint.

Scully continued studying the fluorescent prints through the magnifier. Maybe they'd finally gotten lucky on this case. Maybe this was the break they'd been hoping for: the identity of the second murderer.

"It's the placement of the prints that struck me," Sheherlis went on.

Scully didn't see anything unusual in that. "They're oriented where someone would have gripped the knife," she observed.

Sheherlis nodded. "Which is why I thought I had your guy. Except . . ." Sheherlis pulled off her goggles. "I wasn't as lucky as I thought. I ran the prints against the NCIC database," she said, referring to the files of the National Crime Information Center.

Now Scully removed her own goggles, regarding the scientist curiously.

"But your message said you identified them—"

"Oh, I did," Sheherlis assured her. "Turns out he's one of our own people."

"An FBI agent?" Scully asked. Of course the prints of everyone who worked for the Bureau were on file, but—

"Your partner," Sheherlis said.

Scully couldn't believe she'd heard correctly. "These are Mulder's prints? Are you sure?"

"I double-checked," Sheherlis said. She looked at Scully as if surprised by her reaction. "Well, why? I assumed he must have been the one who recovered the knife at the crime scene."

"Excuse me," Scully said, and hurried out of the lab before Sheherlis could ask more questions.

Twenty minutes later, Scully was deep inside FBI headquarters' Evidence Room L–7. Rows of metal shelves lined the room, stacked from floor to ceiling. And each shelf held dozens of cardboard cartons filled with evidence from thefts and kidnappings, rapes and murders. Everything was labeled and sorted, as if the worst that humans were capable of could really be so neatly contained.

Scully followed a bespectacled young agent down one of the far aisles. She still couldn't believe the news from Sheherlis. Even if Mulder had been the one to recover the knife at the crime scene, he was too meticulous an agent to get his fingerprints all over it. Mulder was always careful to use latex gloves before handling a piece of evidence. Granted, he hadn't had much sleep lately, but still . . . the question remained: When and why had he gotten hold of the knife?

The young agent finally stopped and pulled a white cardboard carton from one of the upper shelves—the evidence box from Mostow's case. A phone rang and he said hurriedly, "There's a table up front where you can examine the contents."

"That's okay," Scully said. "You can just set it down on the floor."

He shrugged as the phone rang again. "I need to get that," he said apologetically and hurried off, leaving Scully alone with the box in the middle of the aisle.

Good, Scully thought. She'd rather not have anyone watching now. She knelt and took a breath, dreading what she might find—or not find—inside. Then she opened the box and rummaged through the contents. Strands of hair from one of the victims, found in Mostow's apartment. Fibers from Mostow's jacket found under another victim's nails. One of Mostow's charcoal pencils and a drawing of a gargoyle left in the third victim's car.

Scully felt a wave of dread go through her as she found what she was looking for. Slowly, she removed an empty plastic bag. The label on it read: MOSTOW, JOHN L. L–7 #2257 KNIFE.

Scully sat back on her heels, looking at the

empty bag in her hand, trying to process her discovery. Had Mulder taken the knife? There would be a record of him signing it out, if he had. Unless he hadn't bothered to sign it out. Scully didn't want to think about that one. If Mulder had removed a piece of evidence without authorization, and if Skinner ever found out . . .

"Excuse me. Agent Scully?"

She tensed at the sound of the young agent's voice. He'd reappeared behind her at the head of the aisle. Did he know about Mulder? she wondered.

"That phone call was for you," the young man reported. "Assistant Director Skinner has asked to see you right away."

Chapter Thirteen

Scully knocked on the door of Skinner's office and waited. She was not looking forward to this meeting with her supervisor. She and Mulder had had their run-ins with Skinner before. An ex-Marine, Skinner was a tough, demanding boss who played by the rules. He was not fond of Mulder's unorthodox investigative methods. Beyond that, Skinner was notoriously difficult to read; Scully never knew whether he was about to commend her or read her the riot act. In the past he'd done both. He could, she knew, be a formidable foe. And she knew that she had to be as careful with him as she was with any suspect.

"Come in," Skinner called.

Scully entered the large, spare office. An American flag, a flag with the emblem of the FBI, and a picture of the president of the United States were the only decorations. All were reminders of Skinner's single-minded devotion to serving his country. Skinner himself was a middle-aged man with wire-rimmed glasses and an erect bearing that still identified him as a military man.

"You wanted to see me, sir?" Scully asked, hoping she didn't look nearly as apprehensive as she felt.

"Yes, sit down." As usual, Skinner got right to the point. "I heard they found you in Evidence. I assume you were looking for the murder weapon in this Mostow case."

"Yes, sir."

"Did you find it?"

Scully shook her head. "No, sir."

Skinner's line of questioning was planned and precise, like a prosecuting attorney about to nail a felon. "Is it your opinion that the missing evidence was the same weapon that you found outside Mostow's building earlier today?"

"I'm not absolutely certain," Scully said.

"But Agent Mulder's prints were found on it."

"Yes, sir," Scully said, wondering how he'd learned this so quickly.

Skinner stared at Scully for a moment, and she knew that he knew exactly what she was doing: providing the briefest possible answers—giving him only the smallest amount of information necessary to avoid a charge of insubordination.

"Have you seen Agent Mulder or spoken to him about this?" Skinner went on.

"No, sir."

"Do you have any insight into Agent Mulder's current disposition or mental state?" he asked.

Scully answered quickly and carefully. "I know Agent Mulder is working very hard on this case. At your request, sir," she reminded him.

Skinner ignored her barb. "Are you worried about him, Agent Scully?"

"No, sir," Scully said, lying to Skinner for the first time.

Skinner rested his chin on his fist and his eyes seemed to bore right through her. He asked again, but this time he gave her the protection she needed. "Off the record?"

Scully hesitated, then concern spread across her face, betraying her real feelings.

Skinner nodded, having gotten the answer he sought. "So am I," he said softly.

Mulder once again was in Mostow's sculpture studio. Outside, the wind howled. Moonlight filtered in through the grimy skylight, illuminating the gargoyles that had been made even creepier by their mutilations at the hands of the FBI. Some were perched atop their steel rods, eviscerated. Others lay on the ground.

Mulder stood in the darkness, guiding his flashlight beam around the room. Though the old factory building was unheated and numbingly cold, perspiration covered his face.

He couldn't let it go. There was something here he had to find. His light beam played against the grotesque faces, casting eerie shadows that danced and flickered across the walls and climbed the ceiling above him.

The place was starting to get to him. Mulder knew it was crazy, but he was beginning to feel as though the grotesque faces were watching him. His heart was pounding; the shadows of the gargoyles loomed over him, threatening. . . .

Suddenly, Mulder glanced down and noticed a shadow stretching past him on the floor. He wheeled around and was tackled hard from behind. His flashlight bounced against the floor in a macabre dance.

Mulder fought fiercely, turning in the monster's grip and trying to free his hand from the clawed hand of his attacker. It was the same creature who had assaulted him before: a being with a man's body in a dark jacket and pants and a gargoyle's monstrous face.

Mulder twisted his head to the side and saw the young agent, Nemhauser—Patterson's new favorite—standing just behind his attacker, watching impassively. And across from Nemhauser stood Patterson—also watching.

With a tremendous effort, Mulder finally worked his arm free and realized that he held the knife—the matte knife—in his own hand. He swiped at his attacker with the blade. But he wasn't fast enough or strong enough. The gargoyle also held a blade in his own hand. And he brought it down, slicing across Mulder's face. . . .

Chapter Fourteen

Mulder started awake, spilling to the floor the contents of the file folder on his chest. He was home. In his own apartment. He'd fallen asleep on the couch in his study while going over the case for the umpteenth time. He hadn't even taken off his tie. He felt his pounding heart start to slow as he sat up and rubbed his eyes.

The gargoyle's attack, Nemhauser and Patterson looking on—it was all just a dream, he realized. He wasn't sure exactly what it meant or was trying to tell him. And yet Mulder knew that every dream held a kernel of truth. It was time to find out what that truth was.

He grabbed his coat and headed out of the

apartment. Outside, the wind whistled and tree limbs swayed, throwing moonlit shadows against the walls of Mulder's study—which were still covered with Mostow's gargoyle drawings.

Mulder parked his car near the loading docks of Mostow's building. It felt like no time had passed since the night before—since the gargoyle had attacked him in reality.

He got out and quickly crossed to the abandoned factory, his hands in his pockets. The night air was bitingly cold. Steam rose from other buildings in the neighborhood.

Mulder unlocked the outside door, then ascended the creaky stairs, flashlight in hand. He felt his heart pounding as he neared Mostow's lair, partly with the memory of last night's attack, partly with the memory of the dream. It had felt so real.

He pushed open Mostow's door, letting his flashlight beam precede him into the dark space. He moved slowly, purposefully, into the main room, then through the rough-hewn doorway into the gruesome gallery that had been hidden.

The skin along the back of his neck prickled as he entered the sculpture studio. He searched the room with his light, and the shadows of the grotesques began to play along the walls. This felt so much like the dream, Mulder half expected his nightmare to repeat itself. To become real. Any second now, he'd see a shadow sweep across the floor and—

And then Mulder saw something that stopped him in his tracks. A clay gargoyle illuminated by the bright beam of his light. Staring at him. Sitting on the same pallet where Mulder had been working with the clay just one night ago. Unlike the other sculptures, however, this gargoyle was whole. Fresh.

It hadn't been here the night before.

A wave of dread went through Mulder as he approached the new sculpture. Head, chest, and shoulders; the bust had no arms. Mulder studied it closely. Though it was similar to the other figures, there was something different, something almost sad in its expression. He touched it. The clay was still wet.

Then Mulder's attention was drawn by a lapping, scratching sound. He guided his flashlight, searching for the source of the sound, and finally saw the longhaired black cat. The cat saw him as well, and darted across the floor into the shadows.

Abandoning the pool of dark red blood that it had been drinking.

Mulder's light followed the trail of blood. It pooled, then tapered off into a rivulet, which disappeared behind a stack of crates.

He stepped cautiously around the crates, following the stream. A human hand lay on the floor, its fingers gnarled in death, clawing at the floorboards.

Fighting back nausea, Mulder used his light to trace the length of the arm, still in its shirtsleeve. The cotton sleeve was torn and soaked with blood. The arm had been severed at the shoulder.

Chapter Fifteen

As Scully rode the elevator to her apartment, her mind was still on the case. She'd never been very good at leaving work behind at the office, and this case was bothering her more than most. None of the usual investigative tools seemed to be working. Fingerprints, stakeouts, and careful accumulation of evidence had gotten them John Mostow. But the murders hadn't stopped, and as far as she could tell, no one was any closer to stopping them. In fact, the only new bit of evidence they had—the prints on the knife—led straight to Fox Mulder.

On top of that, the interview with Skinner had completely unnerved her. Walter S. Skinner was not a man to worry needlessly. If he was concerned about Mulder, chances were he'd take action. Scully wondered whether he'd yank them from the case. If he could even find Mulder to yank, that is. She still hadn't heard from her partner, and that worried her most of all.

She opened the door to her apartment and saw the red light on her answering machine blinking. *Maybe it's Mulder,* she thought as she hung up her coat.

She hurried to the machine, pressed the PLAY button, and waited impatiently as the tape rewound. Then the gray box beeped and the hushed, urgent voice of Agent Nemhauser could be heard through the tinny speaker. "Yeah, this is Greg Nemhauser. Please call me right away at 555–0143. I need to talk to you right away about a possible—"

His voice cut off suddenly, the line inexplicably disconnected.

Concerned, Scully hit the REWIND button, then picked up her phone and dialed Nemhauser's number. . . .

• • •

In Mostow's sculpture studio, Mulder started at the sound of a cell phone ringing. The pitch was too high to be his own phone. Mulder began to search through the dark room as the high, tinny ring continued, like an annoying insect. It didn't make sense, Mulder told himself. Mostow wouldn't have had a cell phone. He could barely afford a blanket.

Mulder aimed his flashlight along the floor, into a supply bin, inside a plastic bucket, and then around the grotesque sculptures. He kept searching, his desperation underscored by the insistent ringing.

Finally, his beam lit on a man's coat crumpled on one of the work tables. The ringing got louder and louder as Mulder moved toward it. He picked up the torn coat and found the phone in a pocket.

He pulled out the antenna and quickly pressed the ON button. "Hello?"

"Mulder?" a surprised female voice asked.

"Scully?"

"Where are you?"

"I'm in Mostow's studio."

"Are you with Nemhauser?" Scully asked.

The question took Mulder by surprise. "No. Should I be?"

"Well, that's who I was calling," Scully explained. "He left this number on my answering machine. He said he had to talk to me."

Mulder said nothing as he stared at the coat in his hands with a sickening realization. It was Nemhauser's cell phone, which meant this was Nemhauser's coat, which meant . . .

"Mulder?"

"Yeah." He wished he hadn't been the one to find the coat. He wished Scully had never called.

"Do you know where he is?"

"I'm not sure," he answered.

Scully could hear the strain in Mulder's voice. What on earth was going on? Was Mulder being straight with her? Was he hiding something? She decided to test him.

"Mulder," she said carefully, "that knife I recovered from outside Mostow's building—I think it's the same one Mostow used."

"What makes you say that?" Mulder asked.

"Because Mostow's was stolen from Evidence."

"When?" Mulder asked.

"I was hoping maybe you could tell me," Scully said. "Your prints are all over it."

Mulder sounded dazed as he said, "Yes, I examined Mostow's knife yesterday, in the Evidence Room."

"Why?" Scully asked.

"Because I wanted to . . . hold it. I wanted to see what it felt like in my hand."

"But why? And why didn't you wear gloves?"

He knew the answer would only make things worse, so he gave her the information that she actually needed. "Look, Scully, I didn't *take* it."

There was a tense silence, and Mulder

knew Scully was weighing how far she could trust him, whether or not she could back him on this one. Scully was a strong, loyal partner, but ultimately she was loyal to her own conscience, and Mulder never expected anything else.

"Okay, Mulder, listen to me carefully," Scully said. "I want you to stay exactly where you are. I'm going to be there in a few minutes. And we're going to work this thing out together. Okay?"

Mulder didn't answer. She was on his side, but she also thought he'd lost it. He could hear it in her voice. His eyes went to the new sculpture. The one whose clay was still damp.

"Mulder?" she asked.

"Yeah . . ." he replied.

The line went dead, leaving Mulder standing there, dazed. He set down Nemhauser's torn coat and put the cell phone on top of it. Dreading what he had to do next, he walked back to the new gargoyle.

He studied the face, the peculiar sad

expression. Feeling sick, he ran his hand over its contours—then began picking at the slimy clay. Gingerly at first, then more aggressively, he began tearing off handfuls of clay. It took only seconds to reveal what he'd feared he'd find: Nemhauser's mutilated face, staring out from behind the death mask.

Chapter Sixteen

As Mulder stood looking at the remains of Greg Nemhauser, a shadow fell across his back. The shadow slid past him and climbed the gargoyle's face—a man's charcoal silhouette in the blue light of the studio. Mulder tensed, pulled his gun, spun around—and saw Patterson behind him.

Mulder eased somewhat, lowering the gun.

"Mulder—," Patterson began.

"What are you doing here?" Mulder asked.

"What are *you* doing here?" Patterson retorted.

But Mulder didn't answer. He followed Patterson's gaze to the limbless, clay-covered torso on the pallet.

"It's Nemhauser," Mulder said.

Patterson moved closer to the sculpture, strangely unaffected by the grisly sight.

Mulder glanced down at Patterson's hands and suddenly understood. "But you already knew that, didn't you?"

Patterson turned on Mulder indignantly. "What's this about?"

"You killed him, Bill. When he suspected it was you." Mulder raised his gun again, training it on Patterson. "You killed Nemhauser."

"Are you out of your mind?" Patterson barked.

An hour ago, Mulder had asked himself the same question. Now, however, he knew the answer. "Not me. Not now."

Patterson edged closer to Mulder. Mulder held his ground.

"Put that gun down," Patterson ordered.

"Not until you tell me what you're doing here," Mulder countered.

"What *I'm* doing here . . . ?" Patterson's voice rose to a shout, then trailed off, as if he found himself unable to answer.

"You don't remember, do you?" Mulder asked. Patterson's confusion was telling. Memory gaps were symptomatic of multiple personality disorder. "Look at your hands," Mulder suggested.

Patterson raised his hands. They were crusted with dried gray clay. He studied them with a puzzled expression. As if they weren't his. His bewildered face reflected the truth of Mulder's statements.

"Now ask yourself," Mulder went on, "what *are* you doing here?"

"I-I'm not sure," Patterson answered. His voice shook and he looked at Mulder helplessly.

And Mulder answered in a voice that was not accusing—simply weary and informed by a certain sympathy.

"You're here because Mostow stole three years of your life. Every day and every night for three years, you lived and dreamed the horror show that was in his head. And I'm *sorry. . . .*"

Patterson was pale and sweating now, his pupils dilated.

"Imagining everything he imagined," Mulder went on. "Sinking deeper and deeper into the ugliness—just like you taught us to do. But when you finally caught him . . . it didn't just go away. All that violence, it stayed alive inside you. You couldn't just lock it up, not the same way you locked up Mostow."

Even as he spoke, Mulder knew he might be pushing Patterson too far. The psychic glue that held him together was dissolving under the force and clarity of Mulder's words.

Mulder saw the madness emerging in Patterson's eyes. Yet he couldn't stop. He'd finally uncovered the truth—and Patterson had to hear it. Before the gargoyle claimed its next victim.

"You didn't *want* to do what you were doing. You wanted to stop it, but you couldn't. Not by yourself. That's why you called on me in the first place. Why you couldn't kill me when you had the chance."

Mulder stopped as he was suddenly hit directly in the eyes by a blinding beam of light.

"Mulder, what the hell are you doing?" Scully demanded.

She stood in the doorway to the studio, her gun trained over the powerful beam of her flashlight.

"Scully, get that light off me!" Mulder said.

"First put the gun down," she countered.

"You don't understand—"

"Then help me understand why you've got a gun on Agent Patterson—," Scully cried.

Without warning, Patterson took advantage of the distraction. He toppled one of the sculpted gargoyles onto Mulder, knocking him down. Unsure of who to trust now, Scully rushed into the room. But, just as quickly, Patterson whirled to face her. He shoved her to the floor and bolted out of the room.

Scully gasped as she landed. The last thing she'd expected was Patterson's attack. Mulder was at her side at once, helping her to her feet.

"Mulder—"

"It's him, Scully." Mulder didn't explain further. He grabbed his gun and took off after Patterson. Scully knew she didn't need to ask any more questions. Seconds later, she was right behind him.

Chapter Seventeen

Patterson darted out of Mostow's studio and into the dark corridor. He ran, his hands in front of him, a look of horror on his face. Instinct guided him as he tore up the stairs and down another hall toward the catwalk. His breath was labored by the time he reached the metal ladder, yet he forced himself up the steep steps. . . .

Mulder raced after Patterson, his gun raised. He could see the beam of Scully's flashlight shining behind him, lighting his way. Even so, Patterson had disappeared from sight almost at once. Mulder, though, had a good idea of where he was headed.

Panic sent adrenaline coursing through Patterson's bloodstream. He broke into another run as he stepped onto the narrow metal bridge. His chest was heaving now, and though the catwalk shook wildly beneath his footsteps, he never let himself slow down. He bolted along its length until he reached the metal door that led outside to the roof. Using his shoulder, he pushed it open—and then disappeared into the heavy shadows of the night. . . .

Mulder and Scully stepped out onto the tar-paper rooftop. Scully scanned the area with her flashlight, taking in the two staggered roofs. A cold wind whipped through the assorted chimneys, ducts, and ventilation machinery. But other than the wind, there was no sound, no sign of movement. Above them, the darkening sky and gathering clouds were the first signs of a storm to come.

The two partners exchanged a look,

silently agreeing to separate. They split up, Mulder jumping down to the lower roof.

Scully searched the upper-level rooftop, her gun trained along her flashlight beam. She stalked quietly, carefully, sidestepping pools of greasy water. She shivered. It was getting colder by the second. Her breath rose in front of her, like a cloud of steam.

She was still trying to take in the fact that Bill Patterson was the second killer. Every bit as sick and dangerous as John Mostow. And now he was somewhere up here, concealed in the shadows, waiting for them. . . .

On the lower roof, Mulder peered into the darkness, behind chimney stacks, around heating ducts, his ears straining to pick up any sound. He heard only the rasp of his own breathing, the pounding of his heart. There was nothing here except for shadows and the night around them.

Seeing nothing, he moved forward a few

steps. He heard a sudden rustle behind him. He spun around. At his sudden movement, a cluster of pigeons suddenly took flight, flapping into the night sky. Mulder felt himself go weak with relief. Mulder eased up, lowered his gun slightly, then climbed a low cinder-block wall onto another level of the roof. It was starting to rain.

He landed softly—and was instantly blind-sided by a dark figure who knocked him flat. His gun landed a few feet away. Mulder reached for the weapon, only to find himself pinned by the creature. Mulder struggled fiercely. He tried to kick, to free a hand and go for its eyes, to twist out of its grasp. But the monster held him with uncanny strength.

Mulder was finally face-to-face with the grotesque, and it was worse—so much worse—than what Mostow had drawn, than what Mulder had seen in his own dreams. The rotting smell, its icy fetid breath, made him gag. The white, masklike face was one of Mostow's sculptures come to life. And the fiery madness in its eyes was unlike anything Mulder had ever seen.

The monster raised its arm. In its hand, grasped between long clawlike talons, a blade flashed. A sliver of blazing white moonlight reflecting against the night's darkness. The blade streaked downward—and Mulder rolled away as the matte knife slashed through his jacket, cutting his arm. Frantically, Mulder scrambled for his gun, only to see the creature reaching for it, too. . . .

Scully heard the sound of a shot below her and raced toward the edge of the roof. "Mulder?" she called. "You okay, Mulder?" She saw a figure silhouetted by the street lamps tumble off a low wall and onto an adjacent rooftop.

"Mulder!" she cried as she quickly descended a ladder onto the lower roof.

Aching, Mulder got to his feet and moved to peer down over the low wall. Breathing hard, he kept his gun aimed at the gargoyle's still form. It lay quietly in the shadows below him, the matte knife still in its grasp.

Scully was the first one to reach the fallen figure. She looked up to see Mulder slowly making his way toward them. "Are you okay?" she called.

Mulder nodded weakly, then joined Scully as she rolled his attacker onto its back. She didn't seem at all surprised to see that it was Bill Patterson.

Mulder stood silently, trying to reconcile Patterson's inert body with the creature who had just tried to kill him. He knew he hadn't imagined it. He was no closer to an explanation than he had been at the beginning of the case, but he was certain that the gargoyle was real. And at different times it had possessed both John Mostow and Bill Patterson.

Scully pressed her fingers to the side of Patterson's neck. "We should call an ambulance," she said. "His pulse is strong."

She began administering CPR as Mulder removed his cell phone from his pocket and dialed. He kept his eyes on Patterson as he spoke. "This is Agent Mulder with the FBI," he began. "I have a man down. . . ."

A few minutes later Mulder put his cell phone away. And that's when he noticed it. High on the ledge of a building just across from the abandoned factory was a weathered stone sculpture. Crusted with ancient grime, the gargoyle sat overlooking the bloody scene, perched like a sentry from hell. Mulder shivered. He had no doubt that something inside the gargoyle was watching. Watching and waiting for the next hapless human to possess. . . .

Chapter Eighteen

Two weeks later, Mulder and Scully, accompanied by a guard and a D.C. Correctional Complex psychiatrist, walked toward Bill Patterson's cell.

They could hear Patterson's screams from the other end of the cellblock.

"He's been screaming day and night," the guard said. "Barely shuts up even to sleep. He's driving the other inmates nuts."

Scully had to smile at the guard's unintentional joke. Then she looked over at the psychiatrist. "So you agree that Agent Patterson suffers from multiple personality disorder?"

"So far, our tests bear that out," he replied cautiously. "Agent Patterson exhibits standard symptoms: memory gaps, at least two personalities vying for control. He also suffers from

125

sociopathy and obsessive neurosis. . . ."

Mulder kept silent. Scully and the prison shrink could apply as many clinical terms as they wanted to Patterson and Mostow, and they'd still only have half the story.

Scully shook her head. "It still amazes me that someone who worked so hard to uphold the law could turn into someone capable of committing acts of such evil."

The psychiatrist nodded. "Yes, I think Patterson's acts were evil, but that doesn't mean *he* is."

"How so?" Mulder asked, suddenly interested.

"When you talk about 'evil,' you imply conscious control," the psychiatrist said. "What you have to understand about serial murderers, like Patterson and Mostow, is that they're being driven by forces that are completely beyond their control."

The guard sighed as they reached Patterson's cell. "Well, whatever's driving him, I just wish it'd shut him up."

Mulder watched as Patterson launched himself against the bars, gripping them with his blackened and bloodied fingers. It was so hard to believe this was the same man he'd met eight years ago—the brilliant, fiercely dedicated agent who devoted his life to getting the monsters off the street.

Patterson's eyes were wild, and his cheeks were streaked with tears. "Are you listening to me?" he screamed. "For God's sake, isn't someone listening to me? I didn't do it. It wasn't me! I-I didn't kill them. *Please!*"

Mulder found himself feeling genuinely sorry for Bill Patterson. He wished there were some way he could relieve his torment—and knew full well that there was none. Patterson was in the grip of forces much stronger than he. The proof was on the back wall of his cell, where the outline of a gargoyle's distorted face appeared—pointed ears, leering grin, manic eyes—every line etched with Patterson's own blood.

• • •

Later that night, Mulder sat in his study, making his final notes on the case. The walls of the room were bare white once again. The drawings of the gargoyles had been taken down. Mulder had only one left, and that one was sitting on his desk.

We work in the dark, he wrote. *We do what we can to battle the evil that would otherwise destroy us.* He let himself think of Patterson as he was eight years ago. *But if a man's character is his fate, this fight is not a choice but a calling.*

Yet sometimes the weight of this burden causes us to falter, breaching the fragile fortress of our mind, allowing the monsters without to turn within.

Mulder took one last look at the drawing of the gargoyle, imagining what it was that Mostow and Patterson saw. *And we are left alone, staring into the abyss . . . into the laughing face of madness.*

Dont Miss the next book in the
X-Files Young Adult Series:

Quarantine
by Les Martin

The vultures circled overhead in the hot blue sky. Big, dark birds with wide wings, scarlet heads, glittering eyes, and cruel beaks.

Dr. Robert Torrence watched them through the trees of the Costa Rican rain forest. As a biologist, he was used to wildlife. But these vultures gave him the creeps. It wasn't only their looks, it was their smarts. They knew what they were doing. They lived on the flesh of the dead, and somewhere close by they sensed dinnertime approaching.

Dr. Torrence forced himself to stop looking at them and got back to what he was doing. With a wooden tongue depressor he pried a piece of loose bark from a tree. Underneath he spied a large black beetle.

"Come to Papa," he said under his breath. Slowly he extended another tongue depressor so as not to scare the bug. After a moment's hesitation, the beetle scurried onto the stick. Dr. Torrence quickly moved it to a clear plastic container in a metal carrying case and dropped the bug inside. Before it could escape, Dr. Torrence slid the top of the compartment closed. He did a quick count. Seventeen specimens.

"Enough for today," Dr. Torrence told himself. He snapped the carrying case shut and wiped sweat from his metal-framed glasses. He scratched the five-day-old beard on his face. What he would do for a shave and hot shower—yet both were three days and two hundred miles away.

Dr. Torrence loaded up his oversized back pack and shouldered it. But before he could start the trek back to his base camp, he heard earsplitting squawking.

He recognized the sound even before he spotted the flock of vultures coming down through the treetops.

There was a feast of death going on nearby.

Dr. Torrence might be bone-weary, but he could not resist taking a look. Studying animal life was not just his profession, it was his passion.

It was easy to find what he was looking for. Vultures made a lot of noise when they were enjoying themselves.

He saw at least twenty of them in a clearing, voraciously ripping apart a carcass with their beaks.

"Shoo! Go away! Shoo!" Dr. Torrence shouted, waving his hands as he moved forward.

With angry cries, the large birds scattered into the air. They did not fly far, however, settling nearby on low hanging branches, as though assuming a deathwatch.

He slipped off his backpack and squatted next to what was left of a large dead boar. While the sight would have turned most people's stomachs, it merely stirred Dr. Torrence's curiosity.

The wild boar was one of the toughest of animals, he knew. You could shoot a charging boar between the eyes and it would keep on coming. What had killed this one?

He peered at its ripped flesh. At first glance he saw only that the vultures had done a good job of tearing it to ribbons. Then he saw something that made him look closer.

Among the open wounds were angry red boils, swelling like balloons. They pulsed in and out, as if they had hearts of their own. Dr. Torrence had seen boils before—but never ones as nasty as these.

Even more interesting, large red-orange beetles were crawling around the boils.

Still squatting, he reached into his backpack and removed his sample case. Then he pulled a pair of latex gloves out of a side pocket and slipped them on.

A moment later, he had one of the beetles stowed in a plastic compartment. Then Dr. Torrence turned back to the carcass.

The boils were gigantic. And they seemed to get even bigger as he watched, their membranes stretching as they pulsed. With one gloved finger, he gently touched the boil nearest to him.

"Ugghhh!" Dr. Torrence grunted as the boil burst, spraying pus across his glasses and into his mouth. Grimacing with disgust, he spit, wiped his lenses on his shirt, and put the glasses back on. He looked at the wound that the boil had left behind—and decided he had seen enough for the moment. He would learn more when he got out of the forest and back to the lab.

But later that evening he was too woozy to capture more than a handful of specimens in the forest. By the time he dragged himself back to his campsite, he was soaked with sweat, despite the evening chill.

Stumbling into his tent he got into his sleeping bag and lay there shivering, then sweating.

His mind fought the waves of darkness that flowed over it. He knew he had to force himself out of his sleeping bag. He had to get to his radio transmitter if it was the last thing he did.

The way he felt, it might be.

He crawled out of his tent, playing the beam of his flashlight ahead of him. He spotted the radio propped against a log near the dying campfire. He turned on the power and adjusted the frequency. Clearing his throat, he spoke as loudly as he could into the mike. His voice was little more than a croak: "BDP Field Base, come in. Field Base, come in please."

No answer.

He decided to wait a moment, then try again.

His face was on fire. His hand went to it and felt the burning hot boils all over it.

He grabbed the mike weakly and took a deep breath. Desperately he gasped out, "This is Dr. Robert Torrence from the Biodiversity Project. I am requesting immediate evacuation from sector zee-one-five."

He paused. He had run out of breath. He sucked air and managed to say, "This is a medical emergency. Repeat. A medical emergency. *Please respond.*"

Torrence struggled to repeat the message but it was no use. He fell back and stared up at the cold moon as he listened to the static of the empty airwaves.

The last picture in his mind's eye was of vultures circling overhead.